Big Brothers
are the
BEST

by Fran Manushkin

illustrated by Kirsten Richards

PICTURE WINDOW BOOKS
a capstone imprint

There's somebody new in our family.
It's a baby!

Our baby is little, and I am big.
I am a big brother!

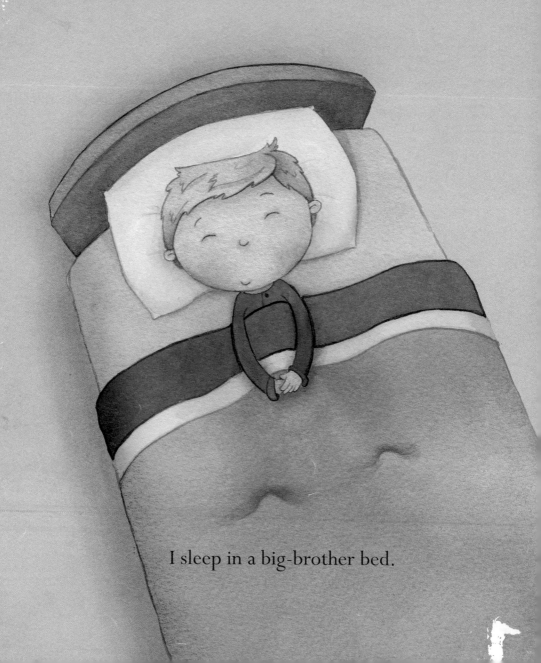

I sleep in a big-brother bed.

Our baby sleeps in a crib.

Little babies are
LOUD and a
little smelly.

When our baby cries, I know why.

The baby's saying,

"It's time for a new diaper."

Or "I'm hungry."

Little babies drink bottles.

Big brothers eat **cupcakes**!

Big brothers are a big help!
Pat-pat-pat — I burp the baby . . .

. . . and put on socks, and hug our baby,
but not too hard.

Sssh! Now our baby is sleeping.
I tell Mommy, "It's hard to be quiet."

"I know," she says. "We can play quiet games inside or noisy games outside."

Big brothers can **yell**,

and kick balls,

and swing upside down.

Once I was little, like the baby.
See the pictures? Mommy and Daddy
took good care of me.

When they are busy with our baby,
I take a trip with my trucks.

Later, it's big-brother time.
Mommy and I build a castle.
Daddy and I **fly!**

I tell the baby, "One day, you'll be big
enough to play with me."
Our baby smiles and holds my finger tight!

"Big brothers are the best," Mommy says.

I am big, for sure!
But I'm still the right size for snuggling on
Mommy's lap . . .

. . . and riding on Daddy's back.

At our house, there are plenty of hugs and kisses for everyone — especially for a **big brother!**

Published by Picture Window Books
A Capstone Imprint
1710 Roe Crest Drive
North Mankato, MN 56003
www.capstonepub.com

Text © 2012 Fran Manushkin
Illustrations © 2012 Picture Window Books

Library of Congress Cataloging-in-Publication Data

Manushkin, Fran.

  Big brothers are the best / by Fran Manushkin; illustrated by Kirsten Richards.

    p. cm.

  Summary: Follows a young boy as he helps to care for the new baby in his family.

  ISBN 978-1-4048-7224-0 (hardcover)

  1. Infants—Juvenile fiction. 2. Brothers—Juvenile fiction. 3. Families—Juvenile fiction. [1. Babies—Fiction. 2. Brothers—Fiction. 3. Family life—Fiction.] I. Richards, Kirsten, ill. II. Title.

  PZ7.M3195Bhi 2012

  813.54—dc23   2011029604

Designer: Emily Harris
Creative Director: Heather Kindseth

Printed and bound in the United States of America, North Mankato, Minnesota.

112012   006967R